WENDY QUILL

TRIES TO GROW A PET

WENDY QUILL

TRIES TO GROW A PET

written by
Wendy Meddour

with drawings by
MINA MAY
(Age 12)

OXFORD
UNIVERSITY PRESS

OXFORD
UNIVERSITY PRESS

Great Clarendon Street, Oxford OX2 6DP
Oxford University Press is a department of the University of Oxford.
It furthers the University's objective of excellence in research, scholarship,
and education by publishing worldwide in

Oxford   New York

Auckland Cape Town Dar es Salaam Hong Kong Karachi
Kuala Lumpur Madrid Melbourne Mexico City Nairobi
New Delhi Shanghai Taipei Toronto

With offices in

Argentina Austria Brazil Chile Czech Republic France Greece
Guatemala Hungary Italy Japan Poland Portugal Singapore
South Korea Switzerland Thailand Turkey Ukraine Vietnam

Oxford is a registered trade mark of Oxford University Press
in the UK and in certain other countries

Text © Wendy Meddour 2014
Illustrations © Mina May 2014

British Library Cataloguing in Publication Data

Data available

ISBN: 978-0-19-279465-9

1 3 5 7 9 10 8 6 4 2

Printed in Great Britain
Paper used in the production of this book is a natural,
recyclable product made from wood grown in sustainable forests
The manufacturing process conforms to the environmental
regulations of the country of origin

~~DEDICATION~~   DISCLAIMER

If any of the characters in
this book (especially my big
brother and sister: Trevor and
Dawn), bear any resemblance
to themselves in real life, please
remember that you are completely
fictional and this is just a
totally surprising coincidence.

Signed:
(writer) *Wendy Meddour*

I'd like to dedicate my drawings to my wonderful
cousins, Annie and Eva. And to my best friend, Claude.

Signed:
(Illustrator) Mina May

ADDITIONAL INFORMATION:
The above-signed would also like to say a HUGE thank
you to Jasmine Richards and Clare Whitston (brilliant
editors), Karen Stewart (brilliant designer), and Penny
Holroyde (brilliant agent)—who loved Wendy Quill as
much as they did and helped them bring her to life!

CONTENTS

Benjamina: in her first ever book!

Mr Hucclecoate: being all headmasterly

Me—Wendy Quill: all excited about MY brand new pets

My very own SPECIAL BAG!

Bathilda Brown: dribbling invisibly

EXPERiMENT 1

WENDY QUILL'S

iNViSiBLE

RUNAWAY DOG

Look! Me in REALLY PROFESSIONAL vet clothes!

When I grow up, I'm going to be a vet. That's why I need a lot of practice. But Mum doesn't like things that poo in the house, and Dad only likes birds that he can't actually find. Which means I'll NEVER be allowed another pet. Not even one. Tiny. Small. Pet.

'What's up, *Wheezy Bird*?' asked Dad (even though my name is actually **WENDY QUILL**). 'You haven't

Pets come in lots of different sizes

3

Dad always calls me Wheezy Bird because of the way I laugh

even touched your

breakfast.'

I twiddled with my not-yet-dirty spoon.

'She wants another pet,' said Woody,

who is my big brother and can completely

read my mind.

This is my actual real family: Mum, Dad, Tawny (sister), Woody (brother) and me

Mum wiggling her
'No More Pets'
finger

'But you've already got a rabbit and
cat,' said Dad. 'What more could you
possibly want?'

'A dog, please,' I answered,
politely.

'We are NOT having a dog,'
said Mum. 'It'll poo in the
house and dribble on the floor.'

A COMPLETELY TRUE, SLIGHTLY SAD, HISTORICAL FACT:

I used to have a hamster called Twitch—but he
died of surprise when our cat jumped on top of
his cage. Dogs are much safer pets because
they actually quite like surprises.

'But Florence Hubert's dog only **dribbles** on the furniture,' I said.

'Exactly,' huffed Mum. Even though it wasn't exactly at all!

'You don't even like dogs,' yawned Tawny (who is actually already a TEENAGER).

'That was last year,' I said. 'I totally **LOVE** dogs now. And I need to try and get a bit of vet practice.'

'Whatever,' said Tawny, flicking through her brand-new horsey magazine.

(Tawny wants to be a showjumper when she grows up and helps 'muck out' at Romelly Pucker's stables. But I'm not

Whoops! Dogs sometimes dribble on books too

6

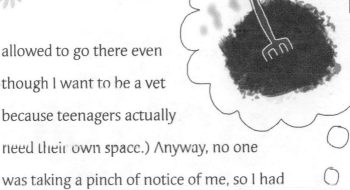

allowed to go there even

though I want to be a vet

because teenagers actually

need their own space.) Anyway, no one

was taking a pinch of notice of me, so I had

to think of something really fast. Suddenly,

I remembered some

VERY IMPORTANT

NEWS on TV! About

lots of wobbly bottoms

getting fat. It gave me an

idea like a FLASH:

'DID YOU KNOW,'

I shouted so that everyone could hear,

Tawny loves 'mucking out' even though she doesn't normally like poo

'DOGS STOP YOU GETTING OH BEASTILY!'

'Oh beastily?' laughed Dad.

'She means "obesity",' said

Woody (reading my mind again).

'What I actually mean is,'

I explained: 'dogs stop

My big brother can read my mind because he's always learning magic tricks

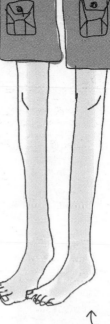

you getting FAT. It's a well-known SCIENTIFIC FACT.'

'But we're not fat,' said Woody, looking at his very stick-y legs.

'How on earth do dogs stop you getting fat?' asked Mum. 'Barricade themselves against the fridge?'

'No,' I said (because that was a silly idea and I don't exactly know what 'barricade' means). 'Dogs stop you getting fat because they make you go for walks—

EVERY SINGLE DAY.'

Woody's legs are sticky like this and not like this

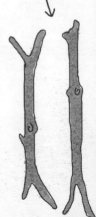

SOME IMPORTANT EVIDENCE:

PROFESSIONAL DOG-WALKING IN LOTS OF WHITE SNOW

PROFESSIONAL DOG-WALKING IN REALLY WET RAIN

PROFESSIONAL DOG-WALKING OVER QUITE TRICKY MOUNTAINS

'Well, in that case,' sniggered Dad,
'I don't think Mrs Quiverly's dog's working
properly!'

'Oh, Arthur! Don't be awful!' laughed
Mum.

ANOTHER VERY TRUE FACT:

Mum always laughs when Dad's being awful.
Even though she probably really shouldn't.

'So can I have one, please?' I said.

'Have what, *Wheezy Bird?*'

asked Dad, forgetfully.

'A DOG,' I said again.

'No, you cannot,' said Mum, 'and that
is that!'

But THAT wasn't THAT because I suddenly had a COMPLETELY AMAZING IDEA all of my own. I put two fingers in my mouth and whistled loudly (which is actually quite tricky to do). Then, I shouted:

Everybody stared but I didn't really notice and quickly ran out of the door.

Florence Hubert was sitting on our wall, waiting for me to come outside and play. Her golden Labrador, Prince, was busy waiting for me too.

'Hi, Florence Hubert,' I said, nicely.

'Hi, Wendy Quill,' she said nicely back.

'BARK,'

said Prince (because he is only a dog).

'Do you want to stroke my dog?' asked Florence Hubert.

'Yes please,' I said. 'Do you want to stroke mine?'

'OK,' she said. 'Where is it?'

My bestest friend Florence Hubert (and her dribbly dog Prince)

'My dog is HERE,' I said, pointing to

the  EXACT SPOT.

'Oh,' said Florence Hubert.

'Her name is **BATHILDA BROWN**,'

I said back. 'She is a chocolate-coloured

retriever.' Then, I stroked Bathilda Brown's

head three times to make her easy to find.

Exact spots
can be tricky
to find

EXACT SPOT

'Watch,' I said. 'She can do tricks.

SIT!' Bathilda Brown sat down straight

away. I gave her a special doggie treat

as a reward—just like a PROPER vet

would. She ate it and dribbled on my knee.

'You know your dog . . .' said Florence

Hubert.

'Yes,' I nodded. 'I know her very well.'

'Is she . . . erm . . . well, sort of . . .

INVISIBLE?'

'Yes,' I said. 'She was the only

INVISIBLE one left in the shop.'

'Wow!' said Florence Hubert, which

is why she is my best friend. 'Shall we take

our dogs for a walk?'

'Yes please,' I said. 'Then we can eat biscuits FOREVER and NEVER get fat.'

So we did. We took Prince and Bathilda Brown down to the brook and let them paddle in the mud. (Bathilda Brown looked happy all over— and I could tell that the brook is definitely her favourite ever place.) Then we played a **REALLY FAMOUS** dog game called 'Chase the Stick'. (Prince was much better at bringing the stick back than Bathilda Brown. But Bathilda Brown was much better at 'Hide and Seek'.)

When we'd finished, we sat down on a bench to try and catch our breaths. (That is

Prince is
AMAZING
at bringing
sticks back

Bathilda Brown
is not quite so
amazing at it.
Yet

16

actually a really hard thing to do because you can't even see them.) It was sunny all over the place and Prince looked all panty and real.

'I **LOVE** Bathilda Brown very much,' I sighed, patting her **INVISIBLE** back. 'But if I'm going to be a PROPER vet, I really need a pet that I can see.'

'But you do actually have a rabbit and a cat, Wendy Quill.'

'Yes, but they are too hide-ative and always run away.'

'Do you want to borrow Prince, then?' asked Florence Hubert, kindly. Prince looked at me with his dribbly-mouth completely wide open.

This is what invisible dog dribble looks like

17

'That is really nice of you, Florence Hubert,' I said. 'But Prince would dribble on the furniture. And Mum doesn't like things that poo in the house.'

'Oh, Prince NEVER does that,' gasped Florence Hubert. 'He's got his own

SPECIAL AREA

in the garden.'

'What's a SPECIAL AREA?' I asked.

'It's the only place that Prince is allowed to poo.'

'Gosh!' I said. 'But what if he

needs to go right now this minute?'

I whispered so that none of

his ears could hear.

Florence Hubert took

something out of her pocket

mysteriously. 'Then I

will have to use this

SPECIAL
BAG'

All dogs have
'special bags'.
It is actually
THE LAW

she said.

'WOW! A SPECIAL BAG?'

I almost shouted. 'I didn't even

know about them!' Bathilda Brown

dribbled on my legs and tried

to make me feel better.

'Are you all right?'

asked Florence Hubert, guessing that I

wasn't at all.

'Not really, Florence Hubert,' I said,

looking at my brand-new watch. 'I mean,

how am I going to be a PROPER vet if I

don't know even about SPECIAL BAGS

and things? And anyway, I think I might be

running out of time to get professional!'

(I got my BRAND-NEW RED WATCH for

Bathilda
Brown's
invisible
dribble on
my legs

20

my birthday, to help me know
EXACTLY how much time I've
got left.)

'But you've got completely AGES,' said
Florence Hubert, who doesn't have a watch
yet. 'Would you like one of my sugar mice?'

She got another bag out of her pocket
(that was NOT actually a **SPECIAL BAG**
at all) and opened it very carefully. The
sugar mice twinkled like shining stars.

Red watches
make you
feel special.
(I'm not
really sure
about green
or blue ones)

IMPORTANT INFORMATION:

IF YOU DON'T ACTUALLY HAVE A BEST FRIEND
YET, FIND ONE WHOSE AUNTY WORKS IN A
SWEET SHOP. THEN, EVEN IF YOU DON'T
LIKE THEM, THEIR POCKETS WILL BE
FULL UP OF NICE THINGS.

I was just about to eat one when I

remembered something

VERY IMPORTANT.

'Florence Hubert!' I said. 'PROPER

vets have to be kind to ALL animals—even

sugar mice.'

'But they're only made of sugar and

pink!' said Florence Hubert. 'And their tails

are just pieces of string.'

'Yes, but . . . ' I was still full up of

doubt. But the mice were still twinkling.

So, very carefully, I bit off a mouse's bottom and crossed all my fingers and toes (which is what you have to do if you want to be COMPLETELY lucky).

It fizzled in my mouth like a dream . . .

Florence Hubert was right! Vets are definitely allowed to eat sugar mice!

My mouth was still fizzling when Florence Hubert shouted in a whisper:

'Quick! Tell Bathilda Brown to hide!'

'Why?' I asked.

'Because LOOK!' pointed Florence Hubert.

Angelina Hardthorpe was coming towards us with a shiny white poodle in

Angelina
Hardthorpe
is the
LEADER of
the 'girly
gang'

her bag. (Angelina Hardthorpe is in the

'girly gang' and they don't really understand

about INVISIBLE dogs and things.)

24

I pushed Bathilda Brown under the bench
and it made Prince become quite jumpative.

Scientific
fact: dogs
are always
jumpative
when they're
upset

'Please keep your dog under control,'
said Angelina Hardthorpe. 'Madame Blanc
really hates loud noise.'

'Sorry,' said Florence Hubert. But Prince
wasn't sorry because he shook his fur and
splattered muddy bits all over the place.

The page before . . . 'Getting Muddy' is Prince's favourite game

'Yuck!' said Angelina Hardthorpe, wiping her poodle clean. 'Your dog's all dirty and he smells.'

'That's only because he's been playing in the brook with Bathilda Brown,' said Florence Hubert, forgetting she wasn't supposed to say anything at all!

'Who's Bathilda Brown?' asked Angelina Hardthorpe.

Florence Hubert looked at me and frowned.

This is how you wipe your poodle clean

I wanted to completely DISAPPEAR.

But I couldn't because this was actually

REAL LIFE! If I told Angelina Hardthorpe

Disappearing is really quite hard. I think I need a bit more practice

about Bathilda Brown, then she would tell the 'girly gang' and they would whisper about me at playtime FOREVER. So I hummed a little tune to my feet and tried to look busy.

'Who's Bathilda Brown?' asked Angelina Hardthorpe again.

'It's Wendy Quill's *INVISIBLE* dog,' said Florence Hubert, letting the secret out.

'An *INVISIBLE* dog!' snorted Angelina Hardthorpe. 'Wait till the "girly gang" hear about this.'

'What *INVISIBLE* dog?' I said, pretending not to know.

Here are my feet—being hummed to

30

'Your INVISIBLE dog, Wendy Quill,' said Angelina Hardthorpe.

'But that would be completely silly,' I said. 'Everybody knows that INVISIBLE dogs don't even exist.'

I heard a little whimper coming from under the bench right behind me. Bathilda Brown was listening to completely

EVERYTHING!

'You two are so weird,' said Angelina Hardthorpe. 'Come on, Madame Blanc. Let's go.' We all watched as Angelina Hardthorpe walked off in her pointy shoes.

'I'm really sorry I lied about my 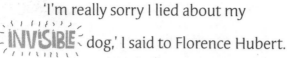 dog,' I said to Florence Hubert.

'And I'm really sorry I told Angelina all about Bathilda Brown,' said Florence Hubert. 'Are we still best friends?'

I grinned and crawled underneath the bench. But something was completely wrong.

'What's the matter?' asked Florence Hubert, curiously.

'It's Bathilda Brown!'

I gasped. 'She's RUN AWAY!'

Tears filled up both of my eyes.

Henna Hussein's mum says that children

do not do bad deeds. Or if they do, it

doesn't actually count. But I had done a

bad deed. And it had counted. I had lied

about Bathilda Brown. And now she'd gone

Losing your invisible dog is probably one of the WORST THINGS in the world

FOR EVER!

At school, I tried to forget about it. But forgetting about your runaway INVISIBLE dog is REALLY tricky to do. Especially when it's ALL YOUR FAULT.

Cloud racing is actually my favourite sport

'Let's play Cloud Racing,' said Florence Hubert (because we actually invented it).

'All right,' I said. 'I'll try.'

We lay on our backs in the tickly grass and looked up at the floating clouds.

'Mine's the one that looks like an elephant,' said Florence Hubert, pointing at a fluffy white lump.

'And mine's the one that looks like . . . oh no . . . it looks like **BATHILDA BROWN!**'

'But you're supposed to be thinking about something else,' said Florence Hubert.

'How can I think about something else when my **INVISIBLE** dog keeps

getting in the way?!' Even though it was

playtime, I began to feel

DOWN IN THE DUMPS.'

But Grandad says LIFE IS TOO

SHORT TO BE **DOWN IN THE**

DUMPS for long. So I tried very

hard to get out. 'I know,' I said, bravely.
'Let's make an **IMPORTANT QUESTIONNAIRE.'**

'What kind of questionnaire?' asked
Florence Hubert.

I think everybody should have a lucky brown-ish pen

I whispered in one of her ears.

'That is an AMAZING IDEA,' said
Florence Hubert (which is why she is my best
friend). 'Shall we write it here? Right now?'

'OK!' I said, quite happily. 'My watch
says we've got some more time.' I got out
my 'Lucky Brown-ish Pen' and started
writing. And my watch was actually right!
We finished it just before the bell!

I should have kept my IMPORTANT QUESTIONNAIRE hidden in my school bag instead of on my desk.

My important
questionnaire
should
have been
exactly here

But I couldn't wait till home-time and wanted to see if it worked.

'What's that?' asked Miss Pinch, who was suddenly just behind me like a ghost.

'Oh, it's just a sort of quite IMPORTANT QUESTIONNAIRE,'

I said, trying to put it away.

'Would you like to share it with the class?' asked Miss Pinch.

'No, thank you,' I said, nicely.

'Come on, Wendy Quill.' Miss Pinch smiled. 'It's not like you to be shy.'

'Sharing' is normally nice. But it's not when Miss Pinch asks you to do it

Miss Pinch doesn't normally smile at me so I coughed like a REAL professional and began at the very start: 'Are you hardworking, Miss Pinch?' I asked.

'Of course,' said Miss Pinch.

Yes

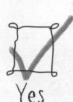

Yes

Yes

I ticked a box.

'And are you very loyal?' I asked again.

'Yes, I am. Very loyal,' said Miss Pinch.

I ticked another box.

'And are you very fussy about your hair?'

'I beg your pardon?' said Miss Pinch.

I looked at Miss Pinch's black

hair. It was tidy and all on

top. So I ticked another

box that said 'YES'.

Then, I followed the

I am
actually
really good
at asking
'very
important
questions'

arrows on my RESULTS page with my finger—just like a PROPER vet would.

'You are a poodle,'
I said, politely.

Miss Pinch
is a perfect
poodle

'A what?' Miss Pinch sort of squeaked.
(Tyler Ainsworth laughed because he
doesn't know much about dogs.)

'A POODLE,' I said again. 'Would
you like me to go back and check?'

41

'Wendy Quill!' shrieked Miss Pinch. 'That's ENOUGH!'

It wasn't exactly the first time that I'd been to the Headmaster's Office. It's not like I'm naughty or anything. But sometimes grown-ups have misunderstandings. And mostly they're all about me.

Headmaster Hucclecoate's office always makes me wobbly inside

The headmaster (who is actually called Mr Hucclecoate) read Miss Pinch's note and told me to sit down on a chair. I did exactly as I was told because good behaviour gets rewards.

'This really won't do, Wendy Quill,' he said, sticking out his bottom lip.

'No. It won't,' I agreed, not liking him being cross at all.

'It seems you told Miss Pinch that she was, I quote, "a poodle".' He wiggled four fingers in the air.

'Yes, I really did,' I said, nodding my head.

43

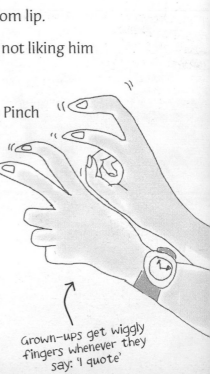

Grown-ups get wiggly fingers whenever they say: 'I quote'

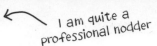
I am quite a professional nodder

'And are you sorry?' asked Mr Hucclecoate (not wiggling his fingers this time).

I thought about it very hard and my cheeks went hot and red.

'The question is,' continued Mr Hucclecoate, 'have you learnt your lesson?'

'Erm . . . I think so,' I said, trying to sound sure.

'And what have you learnt, Wendy Quill?' he asked.

I thought very hard again: 'I have learnt that grown-ups don't actually like knowing what type of dog they are. It is too much of a surprise.'

44

EXPERIMENT 1

Mr Hucclecoate thought I'd got
the answer wrong and made me write
a SORRY letter. But I didn't really mind
because I'm very good at writing letters
and things.

Dear Miss Pinch,

I am very sorry that you are a poodle. (Even though poodles are pretty and have nice hair.) I would like to be a St Bernard's dog. Then I could save people on mountains. But I am not actually hairy enough. So I know EXACTLY how it feels NOT to be what you want to be.

Anyway, I am very sorry indeed. And I promise I will NEVER try to find out what dog you are EVER AGAIN.

Yours faithfully
Wendy Quill (who is actually a sheep dog).

Mr Hucclecoate looked at my letter and made a funny noise. Then, he said: 'I think I'll have to keep this in a drawer.' Which is silly because Miss Pinch doesn't even look in Mr Hucclecoate's drawers. But I didn't actually say anything in case we had another misunderstanding completely by accident.

When I got home, I cleaned out Benjamina's hutch to cheer myself up. (Benjamina is my rabbit and she was called Benjamin until the vet said she wasn't a boy any more because that was just a mistake.) I was sniffing the lovely fresh sawdust when Woody came out,

Nervous rabbits always poo in the wrong place. (This is her first time in a book)

so I told him all about my day. (You know,

about Miss Pinch being a poodle and

Mr Hucclecoate and the SORRY letter.)

I even told him the really awful secret bit

about how I'd been horrid and mean and

scared away my INVISIBLE dog the day

before. But he just smiled and said I was the

Me telling
Woody all
about my
day (by
Benjamina's
bottom)
. . .
WHOOPS!
Another
slightly
nervous
poo!

COOLEST LITTLE SISTER IN THE WORLD.

My very own INVISIBLE POO BAG!

My friends will be totally jealous,' he said. 'Their little sisters NEVER get sent to the headmaster. They just play with dolls.' Then he grinned, all full of pride, and ran into the kitchen to find me my very own **SPECIAL BAG** for **INVISIBLE** dog poo.

(I  **LOVE** my big brother—even though

he sometimes picks his scabs.)

Now all I have to do is wait . . .

Wait for Bathilda Brown to come

home . . .

But she's still not even back yet.

If I stopped right here _____

this chapter would have a

SAD ENDING.

49

But I'm not a **SAD ENDING**

sort of person. So I waited a little bit

more. Then I went inside and had a

HUGE bowl of honeycomb ice-cream!

After that, Woody helped me make a

SPECIAL
AREA

for Benjamina and she got it

COMPLETELY RIGHT first time!

So actually, when you think about it,

this chapter has a very HAPPY ENDING

after all.

~~foot~~ bottom note:
'end' is another word
for 'bottom'

EXPERIMENT 2

WENDY QUILL'S

TINY BORROWED PETS

This chapter is full of little surprises . . .

But they're not actually in my Grandad's shed

Everybody wants to be something when they grow up—even if it's not actually a vet. I know because I found out at Grandad's allotment. 'Did you always want to be a thing-fixer?' I asked, passing him a

REALLY IMPORTANT

screw. (Grandad collects broken things and puts them in his shed.)

'No, Ducky,' laughed Grandad,

'I wanted to be a FIGHTER PILOT.'

'A fighter pilot?' I said. 'But pilots don't

fight. They have to be all nice and smiley.'

'Not in my day,' said Grandad, fiddling

with his upside-down lawnmower.

Upside-down
lawnmowers
looks like
THIS

Mrs Bennett likes leaning over fences

'Ooh! You'd have made a lovely fighter pilot, Pat!' cooed Mrs Bennett. She leaned her top half all over the fence.

'Thank you, Mrs Bennett,' blushed Grandad (even though he's actually called PATRICK and doesn't have a girl's name at all!).

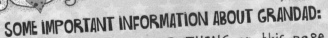

SOME IMPORTANT INFORMATION ABOUT GRANDAD:
Grandad is hearing EVERYTHING on this page because he ALWAYS turns his hearing aid on for me and the 'nice little blonde down the road'. (And the 'nice little blonde' is really Mrs Bennett, even though her hair is white and grey.)

'But why were you a thing-fixer and not a fighter pilot, Grandad?' I asked, curiously.

'Because my legs were too short and I'm blind as a bat without these.' He took off his glasses and blinked.

'Ooh, Pat!' laughed Mrs Bennett, like it was a very good joke. But it wasn't a very good joke because Grandad's legs are too short (because he had RICKETS) and he even wears his glasses in bed!

A SCIENTIFIC FACT ABOUT RICKETS

In the olden days, when everything was black and white, lots of children had RICKETS. RICKETS are when your legs don't grow properly because you're not getting enough food. Grandad's rickety legs are some of those.

'What about you, Mrs Bennett?' asked Grandad. 'What did you want to be as a lass?'

'A ballerina,' giggled Mrs Bennett. 'You know, like that Russian with the lovely pointy toes.'

Suddenly, a voice on the other side of the fence shouted: 'GRANNY, I CAN'T EVEN SEE!' It was Archie Bennett who is actually only five.

'Oh, I forgot all about you,' laughed Mrs Bennett, even though that wasn't actually true. She put Archie Bennett on something tall and his face popped over the fence.

Archie Bennett is good at twizzling yo-yos

'Hello, Archie

Bennett,' I said, nicely.

'Do you know what you

want to be when you

grow up?'

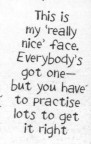

'Yes,' said Archie Bennett.

'What?' I asked, nicely again.

'A SEAHORSE,'

said Archie Bennett.

'A SEAHORSE?'

asked Grandad.

'A SEAHORSE?!'

cried Mrs Bennett.

'A SEAHORSE,'

said Archie Bennett.

This is
my 'really
nice' face.
Everybody's
got one—
but you have
to practise
lots to get
it right

Seahorses look
nice without
even trying

'Why?' I asked (because somebody needed NOT to say 'A SEAHORSE' again).

'Because then I can have babies all by myself,' said Archie Bennett.

'Good grief!' exclaimed Mrs Bennett.

'Blimey,' said Grandad.

Boy seahorses CAN ACTUALLY have babies

But I was actually very impressed.

'It is a COMPLETELY TRUE SCIENTIFIC FACT that male SEAHORSES can have babies,' I nodded. 'I know because I want to be a vet.'

'And I know because I want to be a SEAHORSE,' nodded Archie Bennett.

'Good grief,' said Mrs Bennett again.

Mrs Bennett and Archie
Bennett had to go home
to put the oven on so the
allotment was quiet and
all I could hear were my
thoughts. Most of them
were about being a vet.

'Pass me that spanner,
will you, Duck?' asked
Grandad.

I passed him the
spanner and sighed.
Something inside me felt
wrong.

Here are some
very special vet
thoughts . . .

Grandad
was NEVER
a fighter
pilot

Mrs Bennett
was NEVER
a ballerina!

Archie MIGHT
never be a
seahorse

'What's up?' he asked, all of a wonder.

'Well, the thing is . . . ' I began,

(because Mr Hucclecoate says you should

ALWAYS tell a grown-up) 'if I don't get

some pets to practise on soon, then I'm

going to stay exactly how I am. And if you

were **NEVER** a fighter pilot, and

Mrs Bennett was **NEVER** a ballerina,

and Archie Bennett is **NEVER** actually

going to be a seahorse, then maybe,

just maybe, I'm **NEVER** going to

be a PROPER VET
EVER AT ALL!'

Grandad stood up and patted me

on the head: 'Don't fret, Ducky.

What if I'm
NEVER a
proper vet?!

ALL GOOD THINGS COME TO THOSE WHO WAIT.'

I waited . . . but nothing happened.

I still wasn't a PROFESSIONAL VET

and no good things arrived. So I gazed at

Waiting is
actually
quite tricky
to do

10.22

10.23

10.24

10.25

the mud all dreamily. It would have made a

lovely SPECIAL AREA for Bathilda Brown.

'Tell you what, Duck,' said Grandad,

'shall I let you into a SECRET?'

A scientific diagram of 'How to Grow Things'

'Yes please,' I said (because secrets are my very favourite thing).

A tiny seed

21st MAY

Grandad pulled up a completely new radish. Then he swung it in front of my nose: 'If you want to be HAPPY IN THIS LIFE, Duck, you can't beat GROWING THINGS YOURSELF.'

'GROWING THINGS YOURSELF?' I asked, like it was a question.

A bigger seed

21st JUNE

'You've got it,' said Grandad. 'Growing things yourself. Take these radishes, for example. I borrowed some of Mrs Bennett's tiny seeds. Now look what I've got.' He passed me the radish and smiled.

An ACTUAL REAL radish

21st JULY

At first I was a bit disappointed.
I don't actually like radishes much. But
Grandad is old and wise so I closed my eyes
and thought very HARD.

Growing things yourself . . .

Borrowed tiny seeds . . . .

If you want to
have an AMAZING
IDEA, remember to
close all your eyes →

Suddenly, I knew EXACTLY what he meant.

'Grandad—you're AMAZING!' I laughed, hugging his woolly tank-top tight.

Lucky brown-ish pens are very IMPORTANT

'Right-ho, Duck,' blushed Grandad.

I popped the radish into my pocket and hop-scotched home as fast as I could.

As soon as I got to my bedroom, I went and found my LUCKY BROWN-ISH PEN. (Lucky brown-ish pens are very important if you need to write a **SPECIAL SECRET PLAN**.) This is the one that I actually wrote:

How to GROW A PET ALL BY YOURSELF
by Wendy Quill

1) First, you will need to find some tiny pet seeds. They normally live on scratchy people's heads.

2) Sit next to someone who's got quite a lot already.

3) Then, without them even noticing, rub your head against their head 6 or 4 times.

4) Try to let the seeds get very comfortable.

5) Wait for a scientific amount of time.

6) Suddenly, you will have hundreds of tiny pets all of your own!

Tiny Flo

Titch

Turpin

Bob

Later that night, I put my **SPECIAL SECRET PLAN** under my pillow and tried to go to sleep. But going to sleep isn't easy when you're all full of tinglement (which is a bit like excitement, only much more tingly).

So the night took AGES

and

AGES

Agatha

and

AGES.

Dot

Howard

Dad says it's only a 'proper wash' if you use lots of soap and put the plug in

Then suddenly it stopped and I woke up.

I had a proper wash (with soap) and put on my best grey pinafore. But I didn't wear my sparkly hair clips (even though I **LOVE** them), because I knew that they would just get in the way. That was why my hair was in my porridge.

Me with no hair clips getting in the way

'Go and put your hair clips in, Wendy Quill,' said Mum.

'No, thank you,' I smiled, politely.

'Wendy. Dotterel. Quill,' said Mum (which is what she always calls me when she's cross). 'Go and put your hair clips in NOW.'

'But Mum!' I said.

'No buts,' said Mum.

'But Mum,' said Tawny, 'hair clips are SOOOO LAST SEASON.'

'Are they?' asked Mum.

'Totally,' said Tawny.

I nodded like it was a

COMPLETELY TRUE FACT.

Tawny knows all about 'last season' because she is already a teenager

73

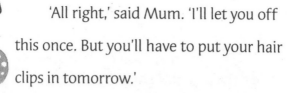

'All right,' said Mum. 'I'll let you off this once. But you'll have to put your hair clips in tomorrow.'

If you're a hair-clip sort of person (who isn't wearing hair clips), then your hair keeps getting in the way. I know because mine really did. But I didn't actually mind because I was TRYING to grow something out of nothing.

Some of the very best hair clips in my special collection

'But where do you find tiny pet seeds?' asked Florence Hubert. 'And how are you going to borrow them?'

'Well, Florence Hubert,' I said, tripping over my bag, 'there's only ONE

person in our class who's ALWAYS

scratchy.' I pointed to his very empty chair.

'Tyler Ainsworth?' She grinned.

This is what
a VERY
EMPTY
CHAIR
looks like

'Tyler Ainsworth.' I completely grinned back.

I normally sit by Florence Hubert (because she is my best friend), but suddenly, another idea popped into my head like a light bulb! 'Florence Hubert,' I said, 'if you go and sit by Laurence Hubert, just for today, then Tyler Ainsworth will have to sit by me. Then my **SPECIAL SECRET PLAN** will DEFINITELY work!'

The VERY EMPTY CHAIR still being VERY EMPTY

'OK,' said Florence Hubert, whispering like a spy.

Lots of minutes passed but the empty chair next to me was still empty.

76

EXPERIMENT 2

Miss Pinch started the register.

Miss Pinch finished the register.

Angelina Hardthorpe took the register to reception.

I don't really know what happened to the register next.

Then, Samuel Bott got a nosebleed.

Then, Samuel Bott had to stand by the sink.

Then, Samuel Bott promised never to pick his nose EVER again.

And THEN,

the classroom door burst wide open.

77

'TYLER AINSWORTH!'

shrieked Miss Pinch.

'YOU'RE LATE!'

'But Miss!' groaned Tyler Ainsworth.

'Florence Hubert's in my place!'

'Then you'll just have to sit by Wendy Quill,' snapped Miss Pinch.

Tyler Ainsworth threw himself onto Florence Hubert's chair and scratched his head lots of times. I couldn't actually

Miss Pinch is very good at SHRIEKING

78

09.21   09.22   09.23

believe it! This was my ONE BIG CHANCE. I was going to GROW SOME PETS ALL BY MYSELF!

'I LOVE the skull on your new pencil case,' I said, shuffling my chair a bit close.

'Get lost, Wendy Quill,' he said back.

'And I LOVE your shark-tooth necklace . . .'

Tyler Ainsworth is the scratchiest sort-of-bully in our school

79

'GET LOST, Wendy Quill!'

hc said again.

'But how can I get lost, Tyler

Ainsworth,' I said, 'when I completely know

where I am?' Before he could think of an

answer (because that was actually quite

a tricky question), I leant forward like a

REAL PROFESSIONAL and rubbed

my hair against his head FOUR times.

Stage 3:
rub your
head against
their head
lots of times

'GET OUT OF MY FACE, WEIRDO!'

yelled Tyler Ainsworth.

'STOP THAT RIGHT NOW!'

screamed Miss Pinch.

'Sorry, Miss Pinch,' I said, even though

I didn't really mean it.

I had to stay in at playtime because Miss

Pinch doesn't like my SORRY LETTERS

and I didn't want to tell her about my

SPECIAL SECRET PLAN. But I didn't

actually mind though because my tiny

borrowed pet seeds needed time . . .

A SCIENTIFIC
AMOUNT OF
TIME PASSES.

Enormous
grown-up nit

Tiny
nit

Medium-sized
nit

Slightly bigger
nit

Teenage
nit

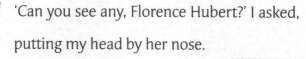

Some of my
best ever
hair clips

'Can you see any, Florence Hubert?' I asked, putting my head by her nose.

'Not even one,' said Florence Hubert, peering in.

'Perhaps you're not looking hard enough?' I said putting my hair clips back in.

'Yes I am!' Florence Hubert nearly huffed.

'Can I have a turn?' asked a voice. It was actually Henna Hussein (which was a complete surprise because she isn't normally the saying-something type).

'Yes, please,' I said.

Henna Hussein stood on her tiptoes and stared very quietly at my hair.

'Are they new glasses, Henna
Huxssein?' I asked. She nodded and stroked
the frame.

'They are beautifully purple,' I sighed.

This is an
actual
proper
NIT CHECK

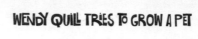

Henna Hussein smiled back. 'What am I looking for, Wendy Quill?' she whispered like a mouse.

'Nits,' I said, kindly.

Henna Hussein slightly gasped.

'Don't worry,' I said. 'Nits are LOVELY. They look like sticky raindrops. And they don't even poo in the house.'

'Oh!' said Henna Hussein, peering in again.

'Have you got a pet?' I asked.

'I'm not allowed any,' she said. 'Dad works nights and Mum's hands are really full.'

Sticky Raindrops Rule!

Florence Hubert is a VERY PROFESSIONAL dog-owner

'What? Not even a dog?' gasped Florence Hubert (who cannot actually live without Prince).

'Not even a fish,' said Henna Hussein.

'Not even a fish!' I slightly shouted.

'That is like a NIGHTMARE!'

This is not even a fish

87

Henna Hussein nodded a lot
because it really was.

Suddenly, I had another ⸜GREAT⸝
⸜IDEA⸝ all at once. 'I know,' I said. 'Why
don't you rub your head against Tyler
Ainsworth's? Then you'll have lots of pets too.'

'I can't,' said Henna Hussein, pointing at
her sky-blue hijab.

'Oh,' I said back. Henna Hussein was
completely right! A sticky nit could NEVER get in
there! I tried to think of how to fix the problem.

'Henna Hussein,' I began, 'are you
allowed to take your hijab off? Just for a
little minute—in the girls' toilet—where no
one else can see?'

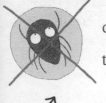

Hijabs
can make
catching
nits quite
tricky

88

'I think so,' she said.

'Come on then!' I grinned and pulled

her by the hand.

SORRY ABOUT THE DOOR BEING SHUT BUT HENNA HUSSEIN IS ONLY ALLOWED TO TAKE HER HIJAB OFF IF IT'S COMPLETELY PRIVATE. BUT IT WON'T TAKE LONG BECAUSE WE'RE ONLY GOING TO RUB OUR HEADS TOGETHER FOR A SCIENTIFIC AMOUNT OF TIME. OH, AND IF YOU HAVEN'T GOT A BRAND-NEW WATCH, THEN JUST STOP AND READ THIS LITTLE POEM AND WE'LL PROBABLY BE TOTALLY FINISHED:

If you want to be a vet
And you need another pet
Try to borrow someone's scratch
Then just wait for them to hatch.

TA DAA!

It was nearly home-time and we still weren't scratching.

Not even a little itch.

Nothing.

Nothing at all.

'I don't think it worked,' said Florence Hubert.

'Of course it did,' I said back.

'It doesn't matter,' said Henna Hussein.

'I didn't really want nits anyway.'

'Don't say that, Henna Hussein!' I said. 'They might hear you. And then they'll run away—just like Bathilda Brown!

And then I'll NEVER be a PROPER
VET AT ALL!'

'Sorry,' said Henna Hussein to my hair.

When I got home, our cat was lying in the
hall looking a little bit dead. But he wasn't
dead. That's just how he always looks. Sort
of spread out and fast asleep. I stroked him
under the chin but he didn't even move.

'Socrates,' I sighed, 'how am I
supposed to get "VET PRACTICE"
when you don't even do a thing?'

He didn't do a thing again.
Not even a purr. So I went outside
to talk to Benjamina.

This is
Socrates,
pretending
to be dead

But as soon as I saw her, I knew she'd

done something really wrong. She was

Rabbit poo

looking straight at me with both of her eyes

and there was rabbit poo all over the place!

'Benjamina!' I cried: 'You haven't

been using your **SPECIAL AREA!**'

She twitched her nose like she didn't

even care!

more
rabbit poo

'Oh, Benjamina,' I said, stroking her

floppy ears, 'I'm NEVER going to be a

PROPER VET now! Bathilda Brown has

run away, my **SPECIAL AREAS** aren't

working and my tiny borrowed pet seeds

didn't hatch!'

Benjamina
not even
caring

'Then grow
a pet in a jam jar,'
said Woody.

'A jam jar?' I asked upwards
(because Woody's legs were dangling
out of a tree).

'Yeah. Mum's got loads
under the sink.'

'What sort?' I asked.

'Marmalade,' grinned
Woody.

'No,' I said, not meaning

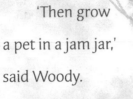

Woody always thinks
his best up trees

PET

A pet that hasn't been thought of!

that at all. 'What sort of pet could

I grow in a jam jar?'

I couldn't think of any that would fit.

'Dunno,' said Woody. 'Whatever

you like. Just put loads of holes in the top.'

IMPORTANT INFORMATION ABOUT HOLES:

You should always put holes in the top of anything that has a pet inside. Otherwise, it might run out of air. But don't make the holes too big. Otherwise, it might just run out.

I scratched my head all thinkatively.

'I still can't think of any,' I said.

'You will,' said Woody, wisely.

Tiny Flo

Turpin

Bob

Titch

Agatha

Dot

94

EXPERIMENT 2

'How long will it take?' I scratched my head again.

'Not TOO long,' said Woody, disappearing into the leaves.

'Oh good,' I grinned, 'I like longs that aren't very too!'

A long line that takes nearly forever

a) ———————————————→

A NOT-too long line (that is exactly just right)

b) ———————————→

Howard is in completely the wrong chapter!

Woody Quill:
who found the
jam jar under
the sink

Florence Hubert:
winking happily

Me—Wendy Quill:
reading stories to
my frogspawn

Black dots:
that are not
even born yet

Slimy Pete:
looking all happy
and proud

PET

THE FROG PRINCE

EXPERIMENT 3
WENDY QUIL
TRIES TO GROW A FROG

Thinking 'jam-jar-thoughts' is actually quite tricky

I was still trying to think about what pet to grow when Miss Pinch made one of her **'Exciting Announcements.'** It was sort of like a miracle:

Miss Pinch's exciting announcements actually look like this

'Today,' she said, 'as part of our PERFECT POND PROJECT, we will be studying the LIFE-CYCLE OF A FROG.'

99

'A frog!' I gasped, all full up of air.

'I beg your pardon, Wendy Quill?' said Miss Pinch.

Sophia Nowitsky is 'gifted and talented'

I opened my mouth to explain but Sophia Nowitsky actually got there first: 'Miss Pinch! Miss Pinch!' she said, like it was a complete emergency: 'Did you know that when a frog swallows a fly, it blinks so hard, that its eyeballs SQUEEZE into its mouth?!'

'Cool!' grunted Tyler Ainsworth (even though he doesn't like girls).

'I know,' smiled Sophia Nowitsky (even though she doesn't like Tyler Ainsworth).

I have very clever eyeballs

'Euch!' said Angelina Hardthorpe.

'And did you know,' said Sophia Nowitsky (because she hadn't actually finished yet), 'that the FROG'S EYEBALLS push the fly completely down its throat?!!'

'Cool,' grunted Tyler Ainsworth.

'Euch!' said Angelina Hardthorpe.

'Thank you, Sophia. Let's move on.'

'But, Miss Pinch,' said Sophia Nowitsky, still waving her hand in the air, 'did you know that FROGS are actually the most DISSECTED animal IN THE WORLD?!'

'What does *dissected* mean?' asked Florence Hubert.

'Gifted and talented' hands are always up

'It's when you pin something down and cut it into pieces.' Tyler Ainsworth did the actions with his hands.

'Well done, Tyler Ainsworth,' I said, because he doesn't normally know big words.

'Get lost, Wendy Quill,' said Tyler Ainsworth.

'Miss Pinch, Miss Pinch, I think I'm going to be sick,' groaned Angelina Hardthorpe.

'And did you know . . . ?' said Sophia Nowitsky, completely ignoring the sick bit.

'I think we've all heard enough, thank you, Sophia,' said Miss Pinch. 'Now, let's focus on the task in hand.'

I think Sophia Nowitsky's hands must get quite tired

Sophia Nowitsky had to sit on her hand to stop it going back up. And Angelina Hardthorpe really *was* sick and even got some bits in her hair! But I tried hard not to notice because growing a frog isn't easy and I needed to know what to do. This is what I actually found out:

~~HOW TO GROW A FROG~~
THE LIFE-CYCLE OF A FROG:
by WENDY QUILL

STAGE 1) Frogspawn looks like BLACK DOTS in jelly and can be found in the slow bits of streams.

STAGE 2) The black dots eat JELLY as their first ever meal (which would be very lovely if it was PROPER jelly. But it isn't. It's the frog sort).

STAGE 3) Suddenly, the black dots turn into TADPOLES with little tails all of their own.

STAGE 4) The tadpoles grow legs and METAMORPHOSIZE into FROGLETS. (METAMORPHOSIZE is hard to say but it makes you sound quite clever. And it just means: 'when one thing changes into something else'— but with a lot more Ms and Os.)

STAGE 5) The FROGLETS' tails fall off— but it doesn't actually hurt.

STAGE 6A) Some of the froglets turn into frogs and live HAPPILY EVER AFTER.

STAGE 6B) Some of the froglets FLOAT UPSIDE DOWN ON THE TOP and actually DIE!

I feel very well, thank you!

'When you've finished your "Life-Cycle of a Frog",' said Miss Pinch, 'please go on to draw a diagram.'

'Is "a diagram" the same as a picture?' whispered Florence Hubert.

'Sort of,' I whispered back. 'Only "diagrams" are MUCH more professional.'

'Oh no!' sighed Florence Hubert,
because she's not really the professional
sort.

'Don't worry,' I said. 'I'll help you.
I'm really good at dead froglets.'

'Thanks, Wendy Quill,' grinned
Florence Hubert. 'I'm glad you're my best
friend.'

This is me—
being good
at dead
froglets

When we'd finished our diagrams, we had

to WAIT FOR THE REST. But waiting for the

rest is quite boring so we

whispered a REALLY

GREAT PLAN.

'Let's meet up

after school,' I said.

'We can find a slow bit

of stream.'

Whoops! *Phew!*

My diagram of
the life cycle
of a frog

'OK,' smiled Florence Hubert. 'Shall I

bring Prince?'

I chewed my lip in a not-sure way.

'Don't you like Prince?' asked Florence

Hubert, sadly.

107

'I completely  Prince,' I said.

'It's just that he ALWAYS eats things he shouldn't.

Especially if they're in jelly.'

'Oh! You mean like frogspawn!' said

Florence Hubert.

I nodded like a PROPER vet would.

'Gosh,' said Florence Hubert wisely.

'I hadn't thought of that. I will DEFINITELY leave

Prince at home.'

Suddenly, I heard a **PANTY** noise on the

other side of the window. (It was *definitely*

a dog sort of pant.) 'Did you hear that?'

I asked (completely forgetting to whisper).

'Hear what?' said Florence Hubert,

forgetting to whisper too.

I listened again.

It was quiet.

The panty noise had all gone.

'Nothing,' I snitted very bravely.

'Be quiet, Wendy Quill,'

said Miss Pinch.

We both went home to 'metamorphosize'
out of our school uniforms. Then, we met

down at the brook.

(Oh, before you metamorphosize too,
you'd better read the next bit first . . .)

My lip
wobbles
when I try
not to cry

109

IMPORTANT INFORMATION FOR ALL FROGSPAWN COLLECTORS:

You will need:

♥ Lots of jam jars WITH VERY IMPORTANT HOLES IN THE TOP.

♥ A bag labelled FROGS ONLY (to carry the jam jars in).

♥ A best friend (or even a brother).

♥ A brook or slow bit of stream.

♥ Shoes that don't mind getting wet.

OK. Now you are completely ready . . .

I looked all around the gurgly brook and
sighed. It was Bathilda Brown's bestest
place in the world—but I couldn't see
her anywhere! (Florence Hubert says
that's one of the trickiest things about
INVISIBLE dogs.) Luckily, frogspawn is
completely see-able and VERY easy to find
if you know all about where to look!

'There's some over there,' I said to
Florence Hubert, pointing to a SLOW BIT
of stream. The black dots in jelly were
sparkling like cling-film in the sun.

'Wow!' sighed Florence
Hubert.

'Wow!' I sighed too.

Black dots
sparkling like
cling-film!

We had a jumpy-up-and-down hug
(because that's what best friends do)—and
took off our sweaty purple trainers, our
AMAZING SENSIBLE SHOES, and
our socks. Then, we did our quietest paddle
over to the other side.

I LOVE
jumpy-up-
and-down
hugs

'My toes are all tingly and cold!' whispered
Florence Hubert.

'And mine,' I whispered back.

'I never knew growing a frog would
be this **exciting**,' said Florence Hubert.

I smiled in an 'I-know' sort of way.
Then, I took the largest jam jar out of my
bag and scooped some black dots in.

All of our
cold, tingly
toes!

Me . . .
doing my very
best scoop

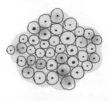

There were lots . . .

And lots . . .

And lots!

'Oh dear!' I said. 'I've got a bit of jelly
in my brand-new, slightly wet watch!'

'Don't worry,' said Florence Hubert.
'My brother's watch can go thirty metres
under the water and still be completely
fine.'

Important
Information:
Try not to
separate
frogspawn
friends

114

'Well, I only did a little splash,' I smiled, wiping the wet bits off. Florence Hubert helped scoop up and soon all the jam jars were full.

'We did it!' said Florence Hubert.

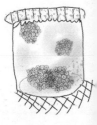

My head felt all fizzy with happiness. 'Yes, we completely did!' I gazed at the black dots bouncing happily in their jars. Then, ever so gently, I put them in my FROGS ONLY bag.

'I think you will make a very good vet, Wendy Quill,' said Florence Hubert.

'Thank you, Florence Hubert,' I said. 'And I think you will make a very good hairdresser.' (Because that's what Florence Hubert wants to be.)

115

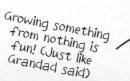

Growing something from nothing is fun! (Just like Grandad said)

Angelina
Hardthorpe
arriving
suddenly!

We were still trying to get our socks on

when, all of a sudden, Angelina Hardthorpe

came past with Madame Blanc. I closed

my eyes and hoped she wouldn't see. But she did.

'What are you two doing?' she asked, in a not very nice way.

'Nothing,' said Florence Hubert, not nicely back.

'It doesn't look like "nothing" to me,' she said.

Trying to make myself disappear

'Well, it *is* nothing,' I said, quite bravely—hiding the FROGS ONLY bag behind my back.

'Oh, I forgot,' sneered Angelina Hardthorpe, 'you like NOTHING, don't you, Wendy Quill? I mean, you like INVISIBLE things, don't you?'

Always be proud of your frogspawn!

'Leave my friend alone,' said Florence Hubert, standing up.

'It's all right, Florence Hubert,' I said, standing up too. 'Angelina Hardthorpe is actually right. I DO like invisible things and I DO have an INVISIBLE DOG. But she's not here any more. She ran away because I said that she didn't exist! But she DOES exist. Her name is

Remember: It's important to STAND UP to bullies

EXPERIMENT 3

BATHILDA BROWN

and she's the

BEST INVISIBLE DOG IN THE WORLD!'

119

Madame Blanc's ears pricked up.

And so did both of mine!

'Did you hear it?' I asked.

'Hear what?' said Florence Hubert.

'You know. That DISTANT
INVISIBLE WOOF!'

'An **INVISIBLE WOOF!**'

laughed Angelina Hardthorpe. 'And

an **INVISIBLE DOG** called Bathilda

Brown! The "girly gang" are SO going to

LOVE this!'

'I don't actually care,' I said.

'Yeah, and I don't care either,' said

Florence Hubert. We looked at each other

and grinned.

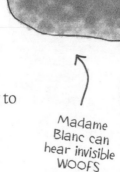

Madame
Blanc can
hear invisible
WOOFS

FROGS
ONLY

'So what are you hiding in that bag?' demanded Angelina Hardthorpe, (not seeing the really BIG label). 'An INVISIBLE picnic?'

'No,' I said, because that would be silly. 'I am actually trying to grow my own frog.'

'A FROG?!' laughed Angelina Hardthorpe. 'What? An INVISIBLE one?'

'No, Angelina Hardthorpe,' said Florence Hubert. 'It's actually the sort that you can see. Do you want to have a look?'

Florence Hubert winked at me lots of times.

This is NOT an invisible picnic

'Are you all right, Florence Hubert?'
I said. 'Your eye has gone all blinketty!'
She winked at me again. Suddenly,
I understood! Florence Hubert was having

Florence
Hubert's eyes
went a bit
all blinketty!

a REALLY BRILLIANT PLAN.

Quickly, I opened my FROGS ONLY bag

and (before Angelina Hardthorpe could say

'NO' or run off in her pointy shoes)

I unscrewed the lid of the biggest jar and
held it right under her nose!

'Eeuuuuch!' groaned Angelina
Hardthorpe. 'That's DISGUSTING!'

'It's completely fresh frogspawn,'
I said. But Angelina Hardthorpe had gone
completely white and was leaning all over
her knees.

Angelina
Hardthorpe
—nearly
being sick!

Eeuuuuch!

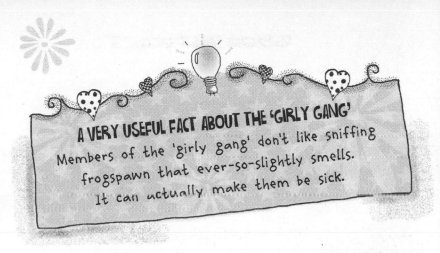

A VERY USEFUL FACT ABOUT THE 'GIRLY GANG'

Members of the 'girly gang' don't like sniffing frogspawn that ever-so-slightly smells. It can actually make them be sick.

'Take those *horrid* things away!' cried Angelina Hardthorpe.

'Bark!' agreed Madame Blanc.

'All right,' I giggled, politely. 'Come on, little black dots. Let's go.'

'You were AMAZING,' said Florence Hubert, smiling all over the place.

'Thank you, Florence Hubert,' I smiled back. 'But it was actually the black dots that SAVED THE DAY.'

The heroes of this story

125

'That is true, Wendy Quill,' said
Florence Hubert.

We walked back home very carefatively
(which is a bit like 'carefully', only with
frogspawn), to make sure that nothing
got broken. And even though we
were very, very slow, it took us
no time at all. (I know because
my watch hands hadn't moved.)

'Will your mum actually
mind about the frogspawn?' asked
Florence Hubert, pushing open
the back door.

'No,' I said. 'Of course
completely not.'

15.35

16.07

This is time moving
very slowly. You can
tell because the hands
haven't moved

EXPERIMENT 3

'But I thought you weren't allowed MORE pets?'

I looked at my jam jars hard. 'That is true, Florence Hubert,' I said. 'But these pets aren't actually born yet. And no one can mind if I LOOK AFTER pets that don't even really exist.'

More pets that I'm really not allowed

'You are right,' said Florence Hubert. 'In a way, they are just like Bathilda Brown.'

'Yes,' I sighed. 'But Bathilda Brown was a lot more dribbly. And very, VERY cute.' Suddenly, I felt a wet patch on my knee. 'Oh no! My black dots are leaking,' I said. 'Let's take them upstairs, quick!'

Mysterious, dribbly patch

The pets that aren't even born yet

The jam jars looked AMAZING on MY SIDE
of the dressing table. (I share a bedroom with
my big sister Tawny and if I put MY things on
HER SIDE, she ALWAYS throws them back.)

TAWNY'S
SIDE

'That is like a **NIGHTMARE!**' said
Florence Hubert, who has a bedroom
ALL OF HER OWN.

Tawny's side
of the
dressing table

'Not really,' I said. 'It's just THE RULE.

And it's fine if you don't forget.'

The black dots bobbled nervously in

their jars.

'Don't worry,' I whispered to them all.

'I WILL NEVER EVER forget.'

Suddenly, Mum shouted up the stairs:

'DO YOU TWO WANT SOME CAKE?'

MY SIDE

My side of the
dressing table

'I DON'T KNOW,' I shouted back.

'Why don't you know?' asked Florence

Hubert. 'We always LOVE cake.'

I scratched my head all thinkatively.

'I know. But would a REAL, PROFESSIONAL,

VET leave new black dots ALL ON THEIR OWN?'

Question: what would a PROFESSIONAL vet do?

'I'm not actually sure,' sighed Florence Hubert.

We stared at the jars on MY SIDE and tried to decide what to do.

'What sort of cake is it?' asked Florence Hubert.

'Lemon cake,' I said. 'I actually made it all by myself.'

'Oh,' said Florence Hubert, sadly. 'I don't like lemon cake.'

'But I forgot to put any lemons in,' I said. 'Do you like *that* sort?'

'I don't know,' said Florence Hubert.

We looked at the jam jars again.

'Florence Hubert,' I said. 'Things that aren't

The *best* lemon cake has forgotten lemons in

actually born don't really need looking
after, do they?'

'No, they really do not, Wendy Quill.'

'So, we don't *really* need to stay here,
do we?'

'No, we really do
not,' said Florence Hubert.

'COME ON,
SLOWCOACHES,'
shouted Mum.

We looked at each other and grinned.

'COMING!'
we both shouted back.

When Mum
shouts she
always shouts
nicely

132

Lemon cake WITHOUT any lemons is actually the BEST sort of cake in the world. And the little black dots were COMPLETELY fine and didn't mind being left on their own at all! Especially as we read them a bedtime story before Florence Hubert went home.

I actually LOVE being a ~~baby-sitter~~ black-dot-sitter

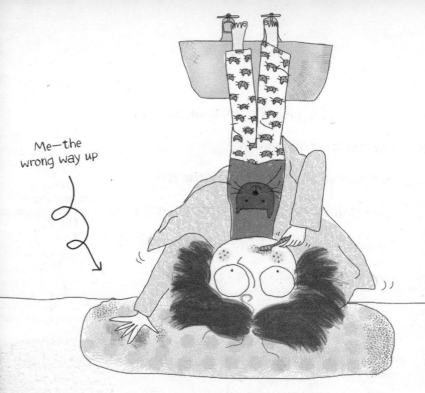

Me—the wrong way up

I was just trying to see if I could brush my teeth upside, down, when Mum shouted:

'Wendy. Dotterel. Quill! What on earth have you got in here?'

I put myself the right way up and wobbily ran to explain:

'It's OK, Mum,' I said. 'They're just black dots—so they're not real, actual pets. And they won't **dribble** on the furniture or poo in the house or anything.'

Me—the right way up

Mum looked at me curiously. Then, she picked up the biggest jam jar and peered inside. 'They're frogs, Wendy Quill,' she said.

'Not yet,' I said. 'Can I keep them? Please?' I pulled my best 'I'll-be-good-forever' face.

Mum sighed. 'I must be soft in the head. But all right then. JUST THIS ONCE.'

'Thanks, Mum.' I hugged her tight.

'But Mum!' yelled Tawny, popping out of completely nowhere. 'You CAN'T let her keep them in MY room! What if my friends find out?'

'Tawny,' tutted Mum, 'what OTHER people think is NOT important.'

'Yeah, but *your* friends won't laugh at you, like, *for ever*.'

'Tawny!' said Mum, all full up of shock.

'Sorry, Mum,' said Tawny. 'But this is MY bedroom.'

'But they're on MY SIDE,' I said.

'I don't care what side they're on,' said Tawny. 'They're GROSS.'

'Tawny!' said Mum. 'You know how much your sister wants to be a vet. She's only trying to get a bit of practice.'

'I know,' said Tawny. 'But Mum . . . *please*. Make her take them away.'

'No,' said Mum, 'my decision is final. I'm afraid that the jam jars have to stay.' (Which sounded like a bad thing, but it wasn't.)

GROWING your own FROG is AMAZING (and much easier than growing pets from someone else's head). You see, black dots DON'T actually stay black dots for very long! Some of them grow swishy tails, and

I love it when my jam jars can STAY!

some of them get wiggly legs! And soon, the jam jars (WITH VERY IMPORTANT HOLES IN THE TOP) weren't even big enough! Mum gave me a spare washing-up bowl and Woody helped me fill it with rocks and mud and water. Then, we

Woody is actually VERY helpful

poured in the BRAND NEW TADPOLES

and watched them all swim about.

Even Tawny said it was AWESOME.

Some of the tiny ones mysteriously

DISAPPEARED but some of the bigger

ones actually turned into REAL LIFE

FROGLETS!!!

This is my favourite tadpoley thing—the bit when they get little wibbly legs

A NOT-SURE FACT (FROM MY BROTHER)

Woody says that the big ones ATE the little ones because I didn't give them any meat and that's what turned them into CANNIBALS!!! But I didn't see the big ones eat anybody else and anyway, I'm not allowed meat on MY SIDE of the bedroom.

'Shall we give them names?' asked
Tawny, trying her best to help.

'I already have,' I said—showing her
my favourites—**BEATRIX** and **SLIMY PETE**.

'Aw, they're cute. But can I call that
bouncy one **BEYONCE**?' It was a froglet with
big, blinky eyes.

'And can I call that fat one **BATMAN**?'
asked Woody—pointing to a black
tadpole with new legs.

'Yes, of course you can,'
I said, because those names
were better than **DOREEN** and
DAVID and actually seemed
just right.

My big
sister knows
all about
names

DIAGRAM OF SOME OF MY FAVOURITE TADPOLES AND FROGLETS (WITH THEIR CORRECT AND ACTUAL NAMES)

BEATRIX

SLIMY PETE

BEYONCE

WRIGGLE

DOTTY

BATMAN

Sometimes, I gave **BEATRIX**, **BEYONCE**, **BATMAN**, and **SLIMY PETE** a new rock to sit on. And sometimes I just told them about my day. (Even Socrates liked the FROGLETS so much that we had to keep the door always shut.) But then, Tawny started to change her mind.

'They're beginning to smell!' she moaned.

Some bottles can stop teenagers smelling whiffity

'That is because they are growing up,' I said, looking at the bottles on HER SIDE. 'Growing up always makes people smell. It is actually a SCIENTIFIC FACT.'

'Mum!' yelled Tawny. *Wheezy Bird* is being really mean!'

'Wendy. Dotterel. Quill,' shouted Mum.

But I wasn't being mean. I was just being true.

Then the bad thing happened . . .

While it was actually happening, I was at Henna Hussein's house, practising AMAZING tricks on her brand new trampoline.

'I wish I could take my hijab off,' she said, bouncing on all of her knees.

'Why?' I asked, curiously. 'It looks really pretty.' It was sparkly and purple and blue.

Mum, shouting nicely again

143

The next page: I am so good at bouncing that I've bounced right off the page

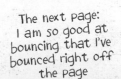

'Because it's getting all itchy,' she said,

scratching it lots of times.

'Oh. That's not your hijab,' I said,

wisely. 'My head's all itchy too.'

'Really?' she asked.

'Yes,' I said. 'I think it's

just what happens

when you're nine.'

I was so busy

bouncing and flipping

backwards that I

COMPLETELY FORGOT

about GROWING A FROG. But when I

got home, I remembered and ran upstairs

to check.

Henna
Hussein
and me
scratching
lots of
times

146

But something was

COMPLETELY WRONG!

'**TAWNY**!'

I slightly screamed.

'**WHERE
HAVE MY
FROGLETS
GONE?**'

'Dunno,' she said, taking off her head-

phones. 'They were just there a minute ago.'

'BUT THEY'RE NOT THERE NOW!'

We both stared at MY SIDE of the

dressing table. It was actually really true.

The washing-up bowl had definitely gone!

We both ran down the stairs.

'Mum! Dad! *Wheezy Bird's*

froglets have TOTALLY VANISHED!' said Tawny.

'COMPLETELY GONE!'

Here is
the GONE
washing-up
bowl

I said.

'Ah. Yes,' said Dad. 'I think you girls had

better sit down.'

'I don't want to sit down,' I said.
'I want to stand up and have my froglets.'

'Well, the thing is . . . ' said Mum.

Suddenly, Mrs Bennett popped
out by the stairs. 'Ooh, here's the little
tinker,' she said, waving a duster at
my face. 'Fancy keeping dirty
water in your bedroom! Whatever
will you think of next? Now then, Mrs
Quill, I'll just go and wipe those skirting
boards down with a damp cloth.'

'Thank you, Mrs Bennett,' said Mum.

Mrs Bennett shuffled off.

'Mum,' asked Tawny. 'Why's Mrs
Bennett wiping things down in our house?'

This is Mrs
Bennett's
ACTUAL,
REAL
duster

'Because she needs a bit of extra
money, love. And I need a bit of extra help.'

'But WHERE'S she put my froglets?'
I asked, not caring about what she wiped.

'Don't be too hard on her, *Wheezy
Bird*,' said Dad.

My completely LOST froglets!!!

'What do you mean?' I asked—not
understanding at all.

'She was only trying to tidy up,' said
Mum.

I chased her down the hall. 'Mrs Bennett,'
I asked, 'where have you put my froglets?'

'Your what-lets?' asked Mrs Bennett.

'She means the washing-up bowl,' said
Tawny.

'Oh, that old thing. I've cleaned it out and put it under the sink.'

'Under the sink!' I gasped, like it was a NIGHTMARE.

'But what about all the water and rocks inside?' asked Tawny.

'Threw them in the garden, of course. Now, where's that pan and brush?' She bustled away to look.

'Tawny!' I almost nearly cried. 'This is a COMPLETE DISASTER! It would NEVER happen to a REAL VET!'

'It's all Mrs Bennett's fault,' said Tawny, scowling at the door.

'You can't blame Mrs Bennett,' whispered

I don't like it when my lip goes wobbly!

Mum. 'Cleaners don't expect to find frogs in bedrooms.'

'Well, I think they really should,' I said.

'Sorry. It's my fault. I should have warned her.' Mum looked a little bit sad.

'It's all right,' I sniffed, even though it completely wasn't!

'That's my girl,' said Dad.

I sniffed again.

'I know,' said Tawny. 'Let's go and find them. They can't have got very far.'

'Oh! You're actually right!' I said. 'They haven't even got used to their legs!'

152

'I THINK I'VE FOUND ONE,' shouted Tawny. 'BUT IT LOOKS A BIT, WELL, SORT OF DEAD!'

Woody ALWAYS tries to sort it all out

'Yeah,' said Woody, jumping out of his favourite tree. 'It's gone all crunchy in the sun!'

'Oh no!' I said, running to the rescue as fast as I could. 'It's **BEATRIX**! What shall we do?' I picked her up and stroked her little dead back.

'Give her to me,' said Woody. 'I'll sort it out.' He grabbed **BEATRIX** and ran inside the house.

'Don't worry, little sis,' said Tawny. 'It's just *ONE OF THOSE THINGS THAT HAPPEN.*'

'That's what Miss Pinch says,' I cried.
'But I didn't think it would happen to
BEATRIX!'

Woody came back all out of breath.

'Where's **BEATRIX**?' I asked.

'In Toilet Heaven,' smiled Woody.

'*Woody!*' yelled Tawny.

'Woody!' I gasped. 'That is really
NOT very nice!'

'Yes it is,' said Woody. 'Froglets
LOVE dirty water. And she'll just end up
in the sea.'

'But everybody knows that frogs don't
even like the sea!'

Suddenly, Florence Hubert came into

This is kind of
what toilet
heaven looks like

our garden. 'What's the matter, Wendy

Quill?' she asked.

'Quite a lot, Florence Hubert,'

I answered back. 'I've LOST my INVISIBLE

dog. I HAVEN'T got Tyler Ainsworth's NITS.

BEATRIX is COMPLETELY DEAD

and now I've lost all my FROGLETS. I'm

NEVER going to be a PROPER vet now!'

I sat on the wall and cried.

'Are you sure you don't want

to be a hairdresser?' asked Florence

Hubert. 'It's much less

tricky. You can even

borrow some of

my clips.'

'No thank you,' I sighed. 'And I've got lots of clips all of my own.'

'Oh,' said Florence Hubert.

'Hey, I think **BATMAN'S** over here!' shouted Woody. He was pointing to somewhere by his feet.

'And I've found **BEYONCE**,' shouted Tawny, pointing to somewhere near hers.

Woody watching Batman bouncing bravely

BATMAN

I ran over carefully to check. They were BOTH completely right. **BATMAN** and **BEYONCE** were bouncing bravely on the lawn!

'Wow!' I said. 'That is AMAZING. They have turned into tiny frogs! But where is **SLIMY PETE**?'

'DOES HE HAVE LOTS OF SPOTS ON HIS BACK?' shouted Florence Hubert.

BEYONCE

Ribbit

'YES, he really does,' I nodded.

'Then I think that he is here by this tree.'

I ran my fastest run to try and see.

'Well done, Florence Hubert!' I slightly

squealed. 'You have found him! It is actually

SLIMY PETE! Hello, **SLIMY PETE!**' I said.

'Ribbit,' said **SLIMY PETE**.

'Did you hear that?' I gasped, excitedly.

'He ribbitted. Just like a REAL FROG

would!!!'

Slimy Pete
is an
ACTUAL,
REAL frog!!!

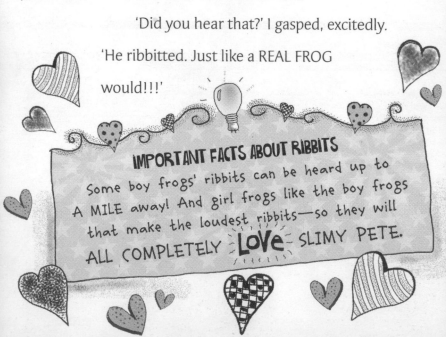

IMPORTANT FACTS ABOUT RIBBITS

Some boy frogs' ribbits can be heard up to A MILE away! And girl frogs like the boy frogs that make the loudest ribbits—so they will ALL COMPLETELY LOVE SLIMY PETE.

'**SLiMY PETE** IS a REAL FROG,' said Tawny.

'See? You've grown one all of your own.'

'You mean she's grown THREE,' winked

Woody, pointing at **BEYONCE** and **BATMAN**.

I blushed, all professionally. I couldn't

actually believe it! I had grown THREE

PERFECT PETS.

'Quick,' I said, picking them up very

carefully and putting them onto my arm.

Three
perfectly
home-grown
pets

'We must rush to the brook and LET THEM GO FREE—just like a PROPER vet would.'

'What? Now?'

'Completely now!' I said. 'Otherwise, they'll go crunchy in the sun! Just like **BEATRIX**! And then they might DIE and EVERYTHING. Come on! It's a

TOTAL EMERGENCY!'

'Oh my goodness,' said Florence Hubert.

'Ribbit!' gasped **SLIMY PETE**.

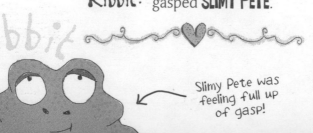

Slimy Pete was feeling full up of gasp!

Woody thinks I might actually become a PROPER vet

It is actually quite tricky to run with froglets, but we made it just in time. They weren't even crunchy at all.

'Go on then,' said Woody.

'LET THEM GO FREE. Just like a PROPER vet would.'

I looked at the gurgly brook. Then I looked at **BATMAN**, **BEYONCE**, and **SLIMY PETE**. 'I'm really not sure I can do it,' I said.

'What do you mean, you're not sure you can do it?' asked Tawny.

'Well, I mean, they're *my* perfect pets. And I've already lost Bathilda Brown. So I don't want to lose any more.'

Here I am!

'But you wouldn't be losing them, Wendy Quill,' said Florence Hubert. 'We know EXACTLY where they are. And remember what happened to BEATRIX . . .'

'Ribbit,' said SLIMY PETE.

'You are right, Florence Hubert!' I said.

I took my biggest and deepest ever breath. Then, I put my arm into the soggy water. BATMAN, BEYONCE, and SLIMY PETE all

Letting my perfect pets go. Just like a proper vet would

wriggled off and kicked their legs—like complete PROFESSIONALS! Then, they disappeared into the bank.

'Goodbye, **BEYONCE**, goodbye, **BATMAN**, goodbye, **SLIMY PETE**,' I waved, trying my very hardest not to cry. (Florence Hubert blew kisses—which is why she is my very best-friend.)

Florence Hubert blowing her best kisses

'Well done, *Wheezy Bird*,' said Tawny.

I looked at the brook and sighed. It wasn't the same without my frogs.

'At least you've still got Benjamina and Socrates,' said Woody, gently ruffling my hair.

A little ruffle

A medium-sized ruffle

An ENORMOUS ruffle

'That is true,' I said. 'But Socrates

just lies about looking a bit dead. And

Benjamina won't sit still.'

'But they do poo in their **SPECIAL**

AREAS,' said Florence Hubert. Woody

ruffled my hair *again*.

I poo in
my own
special
area!

'Woody, what are you doing to my

hair?' I asked, curiously.

'It's all full of funny bits,' he said.

'What do you mean?' I asked, all

fluttery with hope. 'Are the bits like sticky

raindrops?'

'S'pose,' said Woody, ruffling again.

'Oh my goodness,' I slightly shouted.

'My head's been so full of froglets, I almost

So
do
I!

165

nearly forgot! My "**GROWING SOME TINY PETS**" PLAN must have worked!'

'Do you mean you've got nits?' asked Tawny.

Florence Hubert peered in: 'Hundreds and thousands and lots,' she said.

'Euchhh,' said Tawny. 'That's *totally* GROSS.'

'No way,' grinned Woody. 'That's totally COOL.'

'And LOOK!' said Florence Hubert.

HOORAY! My plan to get LOTS of pets worked!

Completely mysterious paw prints!

'What?' groaned Tawny. '*Please* don't let it be fleas!'

'No, Tawny,' said Florence Hubert. 'Not *fleas*. Doggie paw prints. They're right behind you, Wendy Quill. And they go all the way back to your house!'

'Oh yeah,' said Woody, staring at the mud.

I turned round to see. It was actually really true! There were perfect, pretty, dog prints everywhere! It couldn't be . . . ? Could it?

Suddenly, I heard a noise.

There it was again!

Getting louder and LOUDER and LOUDER!

A completely unmistakable INVISIBLE

'Did you hear that?' gasped Florence Hubert.

'Yes, I really did!' I gasped back.

'What are you two on about?' asked Tawny.

Can you see the brand-new dribble?

I *giggle-wheezed* (completely by accident), then wiped the BRAND NEW **dribble** off my face:

'It's my beautiful, runaway,

INVISIBLE dog . . .

BATHILDA BROWN has come

HOME!'

slightly dribbly, very scratchy

THE COMPLETELY HAPPY END

Lot of little surprises

The best surprise IN THE WORLD

EXTRA BITS THAT ARE A TOTAL SURPRISE

BIT ONE:

♥

A VERY IMPORTANT 'WHAT DOG ARE YOU?'
QUESTIONNAIRE

♥ QUESTION 1:

Have you got:

a) smart hair?

b) scruffy hair?

c) floppy hair?

d) stubbly hair?

a

b

c

d

💜 QUESTION 2:

Are you:

a) shy?

b) brave?

c) loyal?

d) noisy?

💜 QUESTION 3:

Do you like:

a) walking nicely?

b) climbing mountains?

c) running about?

d) jumping and bouncing?

♥ QUESTION 4:

Do you eat:

a) delicately?

b) in a dribbly way?

c) quite normally?

d) everything you can find?

♥ QUESTION 5:

Do you like:

a) hairdressers?

b) emergencies?

c) chasing sheep?

d) biting postmen?

TURN OVER FOR THE ANSWERS!

ANSWERS:
If you've got mostly (a)s—you are a poodle;
mostly (b)s—you are a St Bernard dog;
mostly (c)s—you are a sheep dog;
and mostly (d)s—you are a Jack Russell!

CONGRATULATIONS!
I hope you are very happy with what kind of
dog you are.

BiT TWO:

♥

EXCiTiNG THiNGS TO DO WiTH YOUR TADPOLES

❦ ♥ ❦

Tip 1:

Give them completely AMAZING

names—like **BLOB**, **WRiGGLE**, **SYLVESTER**, and

DOTTiE.

Tip 2:

Take them to 'Show and Tell'.

Tip 3:

Feed them pondweed when they're small,

and maybe meat bits when they're big

(so they won't EVER try to eat up all their

friends).

Sylvester
sometimes
tries to
eat his
friends!

Tip 4:

Help them move house

(but remember the

VERY IMPORTANT

HOLES IN

THE TOP).

Tip 5:

Teach them a new language: 'J.U.M.P.'

J. U. M. P.   J. U. M. P.   J. U. M. P.

Tip 6:

Read them bedtime stories.

Me and Florence Hubert reading our black dots bedtime stories

Tip 7:

Tell them ALL your secrets (because tadpoles NEVER, EVER tell).

Tip 8:

Saying goodbye is very tricky. But remember: you have to be brave

When they have got used to their brand new legs, let them go FREE (just like a proper vet would).

ABOUT THE AUTHOR AND THE ILLUSTRATOR

WENDY MEDDOUR wasn't allowed anything that
pooed in the house or dribbled on the furniture
when she was little. (She only had a slightly-
boring hamster and a very sleepy cat). But then,
her beautiful, dribbly, invisible dog arrived!
And she caught some *tiny* borrowed pets.
Oh, and then she grew a frog in a jam jar!
So she had a very happy ending after all.

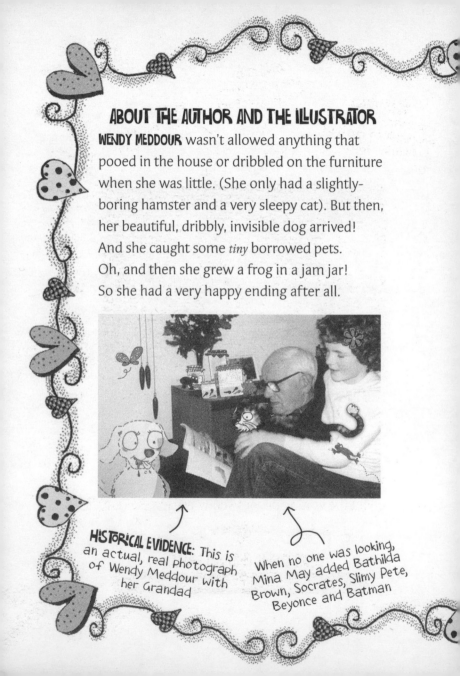

HISTORICAL EVIDENCE: This is
an actual, real photograph
of Wendy Meddour with
her Grandad

When no one was looking,
Mina May added Bathilda
Brown, Socrates, Slimy Pete,
Beyonce and Batman

WENDY QUILL:
the character (that popped into both of their heads)

MINA MAY:
the daughter (and illustrator)

WENDY MEDDOUR:
the mother (and writer)

MINA MAY is Wendy Meddour's twelve-year-old daughter. She is much better at drawing than her mother. She is also better at singing, dancing, mathematics, Arabic, writing, and doing a backwards crab. (But please don't tell anyone about the writing bit, or Wendy will lose her job).

COME OVER AND SAY HELLO:

www.wendymeddour.wordpress.com

LOOK OUT FOR THE NEXT HILARIOUS CAPER:

written by
WENDY MEDDOUR

with drawings by
MINA MAY AGE 12

WENDY QUILL

IS FULL UP OF WRONG

'I didn't actually mean to slightly squish someone!'